The Mystery
of the Bad Luck Curse

**Join Jen and Zeke
in these other exciting
Mystic Lighthouse Mysteries!**

The Mystery of
Dead Man's Curve

The Mystery of
the Dark Lighthouse

Coming Soon:

The Mystery of
the Missing Tiger

The Mystery
of the Bad Luck
Curse

Laura E. Williams

SCHOLASTIC INC.

New York Toronto London Auckland Sydney
Mexico City New Delhi Hong Kong

For Debby Conrad
and Mary Campisi—
writing chums

A Roundtable Press Book

For Roundtable Press, Inc.:
Directors: Julie Merberg, Marsha Melnick, Susan E. Meyer
Project Editor: Meredith Wolf Schizer
Computer Production: Carrie Glidden
Designer: Elissa Stein
Illustrator: Laura Maestro

ISBN 0-439-21727-X

12 11 10 9 8 7 6 5 4 3 2 1   1 2 3 4 5/0

Printed in the U.S.A.
First Scholastic printing, January 2001

Contents

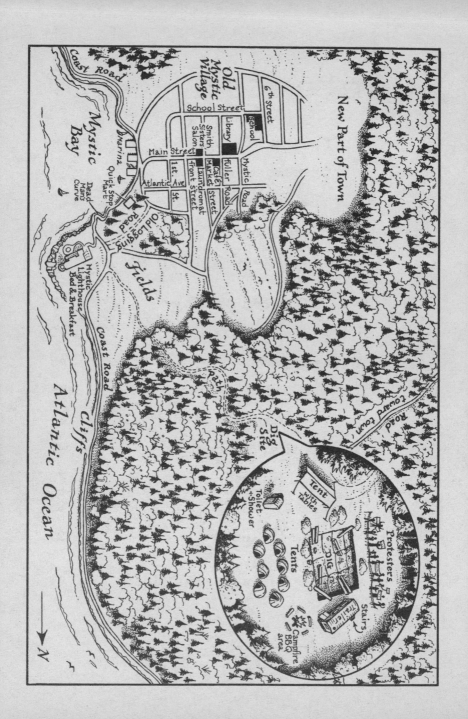

Note to Reader

Welcome to *The Mystery of the Bad Luck Curse*, where YOU solve the mystery. As you read, look for clues pointing to the guilty person or persons. There is a blank suspect sheet in the back of this book. You can make several copies of it to keep track of the clues you find throughout the story. It is the same as the suspect sheets that Jen and Zeke will use later in the story when they try to solve the mystery. Can you solve *The Mystery of the Bad Luck Curse* before they can?

Good luck!

Threats

Zeke looked around the dusty archaeological dig with curiosity. His social studies class was visiting the site on a field trip. Color-coded ropes marked off areas of the site where teams of college students were down on their hands and knees working. They were sifting through the dirt with toothbrushes, small spoons, and things that looked like pasta strainers.

"Looks kinda boring," Jen whispered in her twin brother's ear.

Zeke shrugged. He thought it looked interesting. He raised his hand for the guide's attention. "Have you found anything important yet?" he asked.

The young archaeologist hesitated a moment, raking dirty fingers through his spiky blond hair. "Not much, really. A lot of pottery shards, and some tools and cooking stuff. But we have high hopes for more important discoveries. The settlers who lived here before the town of Mystic was founded all died in the summer of 1698. Legend has it that they were murdered. We're hoping to find some evidence of exactly what happened to them."

Jen shivered, looking at the ground. *Could this be a mass-murder site?* she wondered. She couldn't understand why anyone would want to dig here. It was too gross for her.

"What kind of legend?" asked Tommy, Zeke's best friend from Mystic Middle School.

The guide, who had introduced himself as Michael Durnes at the beginning of the tour, shrugged his broad shoulders uneasily. "It's just an old, silly story. As an archaeologist, I hear a lot of them. It's something about how the ghost of the knife-wielding murderer haunts the place, and if anyone starts digging around, terrible luck will befall the settlers' descendants—the bad luck curse. Silly stuff like that."

Jen and Zeke looked at each other. They knew from experience in their own home—the Mystic Lighthouse—that not all legends were just silly stories. Then something occurred to Jen. "If they were all murdered, how can there be any descendants?" she asked Michael.

"Good question," Michael said, leaning in closer as though he were telling them a secret. "Supposedly, *one* child—a boy—survived."

All of the kids grew quiet, thinking about the poor boy who survived, and about the ghost who could be lurking nearby.

Michael laughed at their sudden seriousness. "Anyway, we haven't seen the ghost, if that's what you're wondering about." He waved his arm toward a campsite. "We all live here on the site, and no one has gone running and screaming into the night."

Zeke looked over at the group of small bubble tents about fifty yards away from the main digging area, along the edge of the woods.

"How cool," Tommy said, admiring their tents. "Do you sleep in sleeping bags and cook over a fire?"

Michael gave him a grin. "Yup, we all have sleeping bags. Except Princess Lori, my assistant, who actually brought a cot, real sheets, and her own pillow. Sometimes we cook over a campfire, but more often we go into town and pick up burgers or pizza."

"How long will you be here?" Tommy asked.

"Until we're done," Michael answered. "Or until Avon University stops paying us to dig." Then he glanced uneasily to the side of the dig where a dozen residents of Mystic, Maine, were picketing the dig.

"Of course, if *they* had their way, we'd be packing up right now."

Jen looked over at the protesters. Most of them were familiar to her from town. Jen and Zeke had lived in Mystic since they were two years old. After their parents died in a car accident, they had moved in with their grandmother's sister, whom they called Aunt Bee. Mystic was a small town, so it was hard not to know everybody. The protesters all carried signs and walked quietly back and forth. One of the bright orange signs read: *Leave the past buried*. Another read: *Go Home! Leave our past alone!*

Why are they so upset about the dig? Jen wondered. *Could it have anything to do with the legend—could all these people be descendants of the murdered victims? Are they all worried about the bad luck curse?*

She turned away from the protesters as the school group moved over to the area that the archaeologists used as their workshop. Under a large, open canopy tent were several long tables, lined up end to end. One table was covered with marked piles of dirt. A college student was sifting through each pile, removing every fragment that looked promising. The student would then label it, identifying the item and the location where it was found, Michael explained. Zeke recognized pieces of bowls and pitchers, and a few things that looked like spoons.

Michael led the group to a table where a young woman was examining objects as she neatly labeled them and lined them up in rows.

"This is Lori Taylor, my assistant," Michael said. "Also known as Princess Lori," he teased.

The young woman briefly glanced up through small wire-rimmed glasses and nodded at the class, then she glared at Michael. Her thick brown hair was pulled back into a tight ponytail and she wore pale pink lipstick. At least five silver bracelets jingled on her wrist, and Jen noticed that her fingernails were polished a shade of violet. Everyone else working on the dig had dirt-caked fingernails.

"She doesn't look too thrilled about her job," Jen whispered to her best friend, Stacey.

"Would you be thrilled about poking around in dirt all day?" Stacey whispered back.

Michael held up a cracked and tattered doll. "One of the things we found is this ceramic doll, obviously brought over from Europe by the settlers."

"Hey, that's Tommy's," someone shouted from the back of the group.

Zeke tried not to laugh. Their teacher, Mr. Rose, glared at the class.

"We label every piece we find—no matter how

small it is—with this special paint to indicate when and where it was found," Michael continued, pointing to a jar of paint at the end of the table. "Then if it's obvious that different pieces of the same bowl have been found, one of us tries to put it back together, using plaster to fill in the missing pieces." Michael held up a squat bowl that had a simple geometric pattern on it, except in the areas where the bone-white plaster held it all together.

Michael continued to show examples, and Jen listened with half an ear while she looked around. Between the work area and the tents were a plastic portable toilet shed off to the side, a makeshift shower that used buckets of water instead of underground plumbing, and a dusty, dark green trailer. Michael had explained earlier that the trailer was the shared office of the two head archaeologists, and that they kept all their important notes and papers there, along with a list of all of the items that had been found and labeled.

While Jen was looking in the direction of the trailer, a short, round man with a thin mustache that was much whiter than his wiry, steel-gray hair charged out of the trailer, slamming the door behind him. A red-haired man stuck his head out of the window and shouted, "I'll be watching you, Murphy, so don't try anything!"

For a second, Michael seemed distracted, but he quickly regained his focus and got the students' attention. Except for Jen's. She watched with interest as the short man named Murphy stomped over to an area of workers, his unruly hair bouncing with each step. Though she was too far away to hear, Jen could tell by the way he waved his arms in the air that he was yelling at the workers. One of the workers started crying and walked away from the site.

"You're fired!" Murphy screamed after her.

Michael had been trying to talk above the commotion, but at the last outburst, he went silent. Everyone turned to look at Murphy as he marched toward Jen and Zeke's class.

Michael cleared his throat. "This is Professor Murphy," he said when the short man reached them. "He's one of the head archaeologists . . . my boss."

Professor Murphy glared at the class, then turned away from them and hissed at Michael, "Get these kids out of here. We have work to do."

Michael shrugged, obviously embarrassed by his boss's behavior. "Luckily, the tour is finished," he said to the class. "I have to get back to work now, but I hear you're off to Burger Buddies for lunch."

As Mr. Rose rounded everyone up and headed for the school bus, Zeke approached Michael and pointed to the fourth long table. It was covered with black plastic.

"What's under there?" he asked.

Michael's eyes darted to the table Zeke was pointing at. "Not much," he said, looking around as though he were nervous. "Nothing important." Zeke's interest perked up even more. Whenever someone told him something was nothing, he *knew* it was *something*. Not wanting to get Michael in any more trouble with his boss, Zeke let his question go unanswered for the time being and ran to catch up with Tommy. "Man, Professor Murphy is a total grouch. I would hate working for him," Zeke said, glancing back at the dig. "That legend sounds pretty interesting, though. Do you think there's anything to it?"

Tommy looked at Zeke. "Knowing you and Jen, you won't rest until you find out."

Zeke laughed. "It would be fun—"

Suddenly someone bumped Zeke hard from behind. "You'll stay out of this, Zeke," a scratchy voice said, "if you know what's good for you!"

The Knife

Zeke whirled around to see Jeremiah Blake glaring at him. "You hear me? Stay out of this!"

Jeremiah stalked away before Zeke had a chance to reply.

"What a jerk," Tommy whispered.

Zeke frowned. "Why would he care?"

"What was that about?" Jen asked her brother, stepping closer. "Did Jeremiah just threaten you?"

"He sure did," Tommy piped up before Zeke could answer. "Told your brother to keep his nose out of it."

"Out of what?"

Zeke finally got to speak. "Out of the legend. I was telling Tommy that it would be fun to investigate the legend when Jeremiah shoved me."

"Weird," Stacey said, crinkling up her plump face.

"I always thought he was a nice guy. Not real outgoing or anything, but nice. His mom owns the Smith Sisters Salon, where my mom gets her hair cut."

Zeke shook his head. "I don't know what his problem is, but if he thinks a little threat like that is going to stop us from checking out the legend, he's wrong!"

The four friends laughed. They knew that nothing would keep Zeke and Jen from investigating a good mystery. They hustled onto the bus, talking about the legend and keeping an eye out for Jeremiah.

By the time the bus arrived at Burger Buddies, Jen and Zeke had decided they had better revisit the dig and do a little digging on their own.

"I want to find out who the red-haired man in the trailer was," Jen commented thoughtfully. "He told Professor Murphy not to try anything. I wonder what that means?"

"And I want to know what was on the table under that black plastic," Zeke said. "Must be something pretty interesting to keep it hidden. Think it's something that could help explain the legend?"

Nobody had an answer for either of them. Pretty soon no one would have been able to answer anyway, because their mouths were stuffed full of double-decker Burger Buddy cheeseburgers and deluxe vinegar fries.

When the bus dropped them off at home after school, Jen and Zeke raced up the long driveway to the Mystic Lighthouse Bed and Breakfast. They had lived there for the past two years, since Aunt Bee bought the old lighthouse and converted it into a home and a B&B. Completely out of breath, Jen reached the large front porch a split second before Zeke.

Aunt Bee opened the front door and stepped out onto the porch, her blue-and-white-flowered skirt swishing in the light breeze off the Atlantic. "I thought I heard you two. Why are you so out of breath?"

Jen punched her fist in the air. "I finally beat Zeke up the hill."

"Because I had a stone in my shoe," Zeke grumbled, trying not to smile. "Just wait till tomorrow."

At that moment, a woman walked briskly out of the B&B. Her heavy shoes and steel-tipped cane rapped sharply on the porch. Her short hair was the same color as the seagulls that kept a watchful eye over the coast.

"This is Mrs. Casely," Aunt Bee said, smiling at the woman. "She's our most recent arrival."

"I'm here for some fresh air," Mrs. Casely said abruptly, her square jaw snapping up and down when she talked. "I think I'll go for a walk."

"There's a really cool path along the bluffs," Zeke offered, pointing across the front yard to where the earth suddenly dropped away to the crashing ocean below. "Just stay on the path—the cliffs are pretty dangerous."

Mrs. Casely frowned. "I think I'll walk a bit inland, if you don't mind," she said, flipping open a tourist map of the area. "Good afternoon." With that, she briskly walked away without looking back.

Zeke stopped his aunt as she was about to go back inside. "After our chores, can we go back to the archaeology dig?"

"Won't you be in the way?" Aunt Bee asked.

"No. We met one of the head assistants today on our field trip. He said anyone can watch if they stay off to the side."

Aunt Bee narrowed her eyes at the twins. "And since when are you two so interested in piles of dirt? It wouldn't have anything to do with the legend, would it?"

Jen opened her eyes wide, trying to look innocent. "There's a legend?"

Aunt Bee laughed. "Now I *know* you're up to something. Okay, go ahead, but be home in time for dinner. Detective Wilson is joining us."

Detective Wilson was retired from the police force, but everyone still called him by his official title. Detective Wilson had been a big help to Aunt Bee ever since her husband, Uncle Cliff, died just before the grand opening of the B&B. He always gave her a hand with things that needed fixing around the lighthouse, and all he ever wanted in return was some of Aunt Bee's famous baking.

The twins rushed through a light cleaning of each of the guest rooms. This week there were only four guests: Mrs. Casely and three other guests who had been studying the local birds for the past week. Jen and Zeke had the cleaning routine down to a science, and it took them no time at all.

As soon as the twins finished their work, they jumped on their bikes and rode along the back path for three miles across open fields and through the forest to the dig. As they neared the area, they could tell something exciting was going on because voices were getting louder. They pedaled faster, and arrived just in time to see Professor Murphy throw a punch at the taller, red-haired man Jen had seen sticking his head out of the trailer earlier in the day. Luckily, he missed.

"Take it back," Professor Murphy shouted at the red-haired man. "You have no right to ruin my reputation!"

"That's right," the man shouted back, leaning down to look Professor Murphy in the eyes, "because you can do that well enough on your own! And if you're the one who's responsible for the missing artifacts, you'll never, ever work another dig!"

Jen and Zeke looked at each other, eyebrows raised. *Missing artifacts? Someone was stealing from the dig?*

All the workers gathered around the two men.

"We'll see who looks better when this dig is finished," Professor Murphy said through clenched teeth. "I've discovered something that will prove what happened to the early settlers once and for all."

The other man's cheeks turned a shade pinker. "What is it? What did you find?" he asked, fiddling with the pair of sunglasses that hung from his neck.

"As if I'd tell you, Frank," Professor Murphy said with a sneer. "I've locked it away where it'll be safe. You'll find out in three days—at the press conference on Sunday, along with the rest of the world!"

Frank, who had looked as tense and angry as Professor Murphy, suddenly relaxed, and the pink flush faded, leaving his cheeks pale with only a scattering of freckles to give them color. He smiled at Murphy. "And you deserve the credit. I only hope my team will find something as outstanding. Now, since we have to work together, let's try not to argue anymore." He held out his large right hand. "Truce?"

Professor Murphy eyed Frank suspiciously. Instead of shaking the taller man's hand, he stomped away.

"That Frank guy sure turned nice in a hurry," Zeke commented under his breath so only Jen could hear.

Jen nodded in agreement. "Like he has a split personality. At least Professor Murphy's not like that."

Zeke smiled at her. "That's for sure. He's just grumpy all the time!"

Someone tapped Zeke on the shoulder and he jerked around to see Lori, Michael's assistant. Jen noticed right away that the young woman had on a clean pair of pale pink shorts and a neatly ironed striped shirt.

"What are you two doing here?" Lori asked. "Interested in becoming archaeologists?"

"Uh, maybe," Zeke stammered.

"Who's that guy?" Jen interjected, pointing to the red-haired man, who was now standing off to the side, his hands thrust into the pockets of his windbreaker. He was staring at the trailer.

"Oh, that's the other head archaeologist, Professor Pruitt. Everyone calls him Frank."

"Do Frank and Professor Murphy always fight like that?" Zeke asked.

Lori smiled. "Oh, that was nothing. Sometimes it

gets *really* exciting. They've been competing against each other for a long time. Neither of them is thrilled to be working with the other."

"Are there really missing artifacts?"

"Yes," Lori admitted. "Little things like spoons and bowl fragments have disappeared. It's actually nothing we can prove because none of the missing items had been labeled or cataloged yet. But even before they're officially labeled, I usually have a pretty good idea of what is here, and I'm sure some of the pieces are missing."

"So all the things that have been labeled are still here?" Zeke asked.

"That's right." Lori brushed a strand of dark hair from her eyes. Her bracelets tinkled like bells.

"What did Professor Murphy find?" Jen asked.

Lori scowled. "I have no idea. He hasn't told anyone. I can understand that he would hide things from Frank, but his own team. . . ." She broke off bitterly. Then she shook her head. "I have to get back to work now. You can hang around; just stay out of the way. Especially out of Professor Murphy's way." She waved and headed off, her ponytail swinging behind her.

Jen and Zeke walked around the perimeter of the dig, being careful not to draw attention to themselves. Soon, they found themselves mixed in with the group of protesters who were chanting, "Go home, leave our past alone! Go home, leave our past alone!"

Zeke smiled at some of the townspeople he recognized, but he didn't linger. He didn't want the protesters to get mad at him or Jen for not joining in. Jen had the same idea and she hustled through the crowd faster than Zeke.

Once clear of the protesters, the twins slowed down and Jen looked back. "Hey, wasn't that Jeremiah's mom leading the protesters?" she asked.

Zeke took a quick look behind him. "That blond lady? It sure looks like her. I wonder who's running the salon while she's up here picketing?"

As they talked, Zeke and Jen neared the four worktables covered with artifacts and dirt. Some workers were whistling or humming while they slowly brushed away one layer of dirt at a time using large, soft brushes.

"That must take forever," Jen said.

One of the workers looked up. "It does. There's a joke that says archaeologists use the smallest tools possible so it will take years and years to finish a dig." He winked at them. "That way they're never out of a job."

Jen and Zeke smiled at him and moved on. "I wonder if Professor Murphy found the murder weapon," Zeke wondered out loud. "Maybe an ax or a knife."

Jen shuddered. "It's all so creepy. I agree with the protesters. I think they should just leave this place alone. Who wants to stir up an old curse?"

"Are you afraid of the ghoooost?" Zeke teased.

"No way," Jen said scornfully.

Zeke was only teasing his sister, but mentioning the ghost of a murderer gave him the chills. He glanced around the dig site uneasily. The sun was already low in the sky, and soon it would set. There was only one more thing he wanted to do before they left. He looked over at the table covered with black plastic. Unfortunately, Professor Murphy and several workers were standing nearby. Zeke frowned with frustration. There was no way he would get a chance to peek under the covering. They would have to come back tomorrow to do that.

"We might as well go home," Zeke announced, taking one last hopeful look at the table, but there were still people near it. "Aunt Bee will have dinner ready."

As they climbed on their bikes, Jen said, "We didn't get any more information about the legend, though."

"Or find out what was under the plastic—" Suddenly, a shrill scream cut through the air. Jen jerked around in time to see Lori scream again. With a shaking hand, she was pointing into the shadows of the surrounding forest just beyond the tents. Jen followed the line of Lori's finger. Her breath snagged in her throat. She reached out and grabbed Zeke's arm.

Zeke stood frozen. "I don't believe it," he croaked. "It's a ghost. The murderer!"

3

Watch Out!

The twins watched in disbelief as the pale shadow seemed to shimmer among the trees. The ghostly figure was wearing old-fashioned dark, billowy pants and a white shirt with full sleeves. Blood dripped down the front of the shirt. A tall, wide-brimmed hat kept the face in shadow. Slowly, the ghost raised its arm. In its pale hand was a long knife. It moaned, then it faded into the trees and disappeared.

For a long moment, everyone stood frozen with fear. Suddenly, Michael charged into the woods. Jen held her breath. She imagined the ghost stabbing Michael with its deadly knife. A few tense moments later, when Michael stepped out from behind one of the trees, she breathed a sigh of relief.

"He must be nuts," she muttered, watching Michael jog back toward the group of workers, who stood frozen in stunned silence.

Zeke's attention was caught suddenly by one of the onlookers. He nudged his sister and pointed. Jen looked over to see Mrs. Casely tapping her cane in the dirt.

"I didn't notice her before," Zeke commented

Jen hadn't, either. "Come on, let's see what she's doing here."

On their bikes, Jen and Zeke swooped to a stop next to Mrs. Casely. She looked startled when she saw them.

"What are you two doing here?" she asked sharply.

"Just looking around," Zeke said, wondering why the woman seemed so upset. "Are you interested in archaeology?"

Mrs. Casely fidgeted with her cane. "Not really. I just followed the path through the woods and ended up here."

"Did you see the ghost?" Jen asked.

Mrs. Casely paled a bit. "That must have been a joke," she said, not sounding completely positive. She moved as if to leave.

"But it was holding a knife—just like the legend." Jen turned to her brother. "That might be what Professor Murphy found and locked away for safekeeping."

"What legend? What did he find?" Suddenly, Mrs. Casely didn't seem so ready to leave.

Zeke motioned toward the dig site. "Professor Murphy found something important, but he won't tell anyone what it is. He locked it up somewhere."

"I think it's probably in the trailer," Jen said, recalling how Frank had stared at the trailer after the fight, as though he were guessing where the object was hidden.

Mrs. Casely looked toward the trailer, her eyes narrowing slightly. "Well, I must be off," she said briskly. Without waiting for the twins to say good-bye, she marched away.

"She could run an army," Jen whispered.

Zeke nodded in agreement. "Come on. Let's see if Michael found any signs of the ghost when he chased after it."

They pedaled over to Michael, where the group of workers surrounding him was just breaking up. Zeke asked Michael what he had seen when he ran into the woods.

Michael shook his head. "I was just telling every-one else that it was gone before I got there. I expected to find something, some clue that it was just a prank." He lifted his empty hands. "But there was nothing."

"Maybe it really *was* a ghost," Jen said. "After all, it was holding a knife, just like the murder weapon. It fits with the legend perfectly."

"You don't really believe that legend, do you?" Michael asked.

"It sounds like the professors do," Jen said, "or why would they be arguing about the dig?"

Michael shoved his hands into the pockets of his jeans. "Well, I guess tempers are running pretty high, and this is a very competitive job. Usually there's only one head archaeologist on a job, but in this case . . ." he trailed off. "Never mind."

"Then what about the secret thing Professor Murphy found? Do you know what it is?" Zeke asked.

Lori joined them before Michael could answer. "That was pretty spooky, wasn't it?" she asked. "I hope it doesn't show up again. It totally scared me."

Michael laughed. "We all heard you scream."

Lori looked annoyed. "I'm so sorry, but it frightened me. I've never seen a ghost before."

Michael's smile turned into a frown. "I was just kidding. What's your problem?"

"I don't have a problem," she snapped. "Unlike some people. So watch what you say, because I know what you're up to!"

Michael glared at her. "Don't pretend to be so innocent yourself, Lori!" Without another word, he walked off in the direction of the tents.

Lori cleared her throat. "Sorry about that. He just thinks he's so great because he's Professor Murphy's number-one assistant and I'm just a measly second assistant. But I'll move up someday!" She shook her head as though to clear it. "Anyway, do you want to come to our barbecue tomorrow night?"

"Sure," Zeke said. "See you then."

Lori nodded at them and started off after Michael.

"Do *any* archaeologists get along?" Jen wondered

out loud. "It seems like they're always arguing with each other."

"You heard Michael. He said archaeology is very competitive." He glanced at Jen. "It's like the girls' soccer league playoffs."

"At least we shake hands before and after every match. I haven't seen anything like that around here."

The twins were reluctant to ride through the forest after the ghost sighting, but it was the fastest way home. So they pedaled as fast as they could along the forest path. They were relieved when they cleared the trees and saw the flashing light in the lighthouse tower off in the distance. *It is always comforting to follow that beacon home*, Jen thought. She was so involved in her own thoughts that she didn't hear the roar of the minibike until it was too late.

"Watch out!" Zeke yelled.

The Legend of the Bad Luck Curse

A hard hand shoved Jen off her bicycle and into a ditch. She rolled twice before she came to a stop. A dark figure was hunched over the handlebars of the minibike as it roared past them. It careened around a bend and was lost from sight.

Jen gasped. If Zeke hadn't pushed her out of the way, the jerk would have run her over. And instead of a bruised shoulder, she could have been killed!

Zeke sat next to Jen in the ditch, where they had both landed with a thud. "Are you okay?"

Jen rubbed her throbbing shoulder. "Just a bump. How about you?"

Zeke frowned. "I'm fine. But when I get my hands on him!" He was so angry, he didn't finish his sentence.

"Him? Who was it?" Jen asked as she stood up, relieved nothing felt broken.

Zeke picked himself up and brushed off the grass and dirt that clung to his pants. "I recognized the bike. That was Jeremiah Blake."

Jen looked confused. "But why? First he shoves you on the field trip, and now this. What's his problem?"

Zeke shook his head. "I have no idea."

Jen climbed back on her bicycle. "Totally weird. He's got something against us, I guess."

The twins carefully made their way back to the B&B. They arrived just in time for dinner.

"I thought I'd have to send the detective out to search for you two," Aunt Bee said, sounding a little worried.

"Sorry," Jen said as she washed her hands at the kitchen sink. She didn't mention the minibike. The twins had agreed not to say anything to their aunt or she might ask them not to go back to the dig. Aunt Bee was very cool, but sometimes she worried too much.

"How is the dig going?" Detective Wilson asked. "Has there been any trouble with the protesters?"

"So far all they're doing is marching around with posters and doing a little chanting," Jen explained, helping herself to a heaping pile of mashed potatoes. "They really don't want the archaeologists there, but there's nothing they can do about it. I guess it's government land, and the government gave the archaeologists permission to dig."

Zeke shrugged. "I don't see what the big deal is. The protesters should just accept it. It's important to find out about history."

"But the archaeologists are digging up the graves of the protesters' ancestors," Jen pointed out.

"I guess I never really thought of it like that," Zeke admitted. "I guess I wouldn't like that, either, but on the other hand, it is interesting. And how would we know about ancient Egypt or Greece if no one had dug? And how about that town in Italy that was buried by volcanic ash when Mt. Vesuvius blew its top?"

"That was Pompeii," Detective Wilson said. "I've been there. What they uncovered is absolutely fascinating. They even found loaves of bread still in the oven. Of course, they were hard as rock," he added, taking a big bite of one of Aunt Bee's warm sourdough rolls.

Aunt Bee smiled and passed Jen the green beans. "Anyway, now you can see why both sides feel so strongly about this dig," she said calmly. "There are always at least two sides to every issue."

"That's true," Jen agreed. "Even the archaeologists, who are supposed to be on the same side, can't seem to get along. All they do is fight."

During the rest of the meal, Jen and Zeke

explained more about the dig, the arguments they had seen, and the ghost sighting.

Detective Wilson frowned. "You say this Michael fellow didn't find anything in the woods?"

Zeke shook his head, scraping the last bit of blueberry cobbler from his plate. "He said it was as if the ghost had just disappeared."

After dinner, the twins went up to Zeke's room, where he flicked on his computer.

"What are you doing?" Jen asked. "I thought we were going to try to figure out what's going on at the dig. So far we have a legend, ghosts, and disappearing artifacts—sounds like a good case for us, right?"

Zeke's fingers danced over the keyboard as he logged onto the Internet. "We *are* on the case. So let's find out more about the legend."

Jen sat down on an extra chair next to her brother's desk. "Will it be on the Internet?"

Zeke grinned. "*Everything* is on the Web!"

Sure enough, a few minutes later, Zeke whooped in victory. "Here it is." He scanned the pages before him, then started reading out loud. " 'Mystic, Maine, USA. The Legend of the Bad Luck Curse. Legend has it that before the quaint town of Mystic, Maine, was formally founded, two dozen people settled on land five miles north of what is now the center of town. But on June 23, 1698, all but one of the settlers disappeared. A four-year-old child was found by two fur trappers wandering through the woods miles from the settlement. The child was crying in fear. When the trappers reached the clearing, they didn't leave the cover of the woods. They said all they could see was that the entire settlement had been wiped out. It is presumed that the child was picking berries in the forest and was overlooked by the band of killers.

"'It is believed that some outlaws may have tried to take over the settlement, but when their plan failed, they killed everyone and fled north.

"'Since then, no one has dared upset this area, as it is said to be haunted by the ghost of one of the killers. It is believed that if anything is disturbed at the site of the murders, terrible luck will befall the descendants of that single boy who was found wandering in the woods.

"'The boy, Obadiah Smith, was the sole survivor and the only one ever to see the ghost. He claimed that the apparition holds a knife and never speaks, but beckons his potential victims to follow him into the woods. It has been said that the ghost is upset that the child escaped and is hoping to seek his revenge on the boy's descendants.'"

Jen shuddered. "How awful! That poor kid."

Zeke nodded thoughtfully. "That was over three hundred years ago, and now the ghost is back, knife and all."

"What was the kid's name again?"

Zeke ran his finger down the screen. "Here. Obadiah Smith."

"But that doesn't explain why Jeremiah Blake is trying to stop us from—" Jen paused. "I don't even know what he's trying to stop us from doing. But he sure is trying hard. What's his problem?"

"I have no idea." Zeke sighed. "I think the only thing to do is talk to Jeremiah and ask him what's going on. I don't know why he would be out to get us."

"Is that a good idea?" Jen asked doubtfully. "He's already proved himself to be dangerous. What will he do to you if you confront him face-to-face?"

Zeke gave her a crooked smile. "Gee, sis, I didn't know you cared so much. But don't worry, I'll be careful. Besides, I'll have you there to protect me."

Jen rolled her eyes. "Oh, great."

~

The next day, Zeke and Jen agreed to meet in the cafeteria at lunchtime to confront Jeremiah.

At 11:45 on the dot, Jen found Zeke by the garbage can, their usual meeting place.

"I haven't seen him yet, have you?" Zeke asked.

Jen scoped out the cafeteria. It was crowded with students.

"Is that him?" she pointed, but when the boy turned around, they saw it was someone else.

"What are you doing?" Stacey asked, squeezing between Jen and Zeke. "Are you on a stakeout?" she teased.

Jen smiled. "Very funny. We're just looking for Jeremiah. Have you seen him?"

Stacey's eyes widened. "Jeremiah Blake?"

Jen nodded, looking around the cafeteria.

"You mean you didn't hear?"

Jen turned to her friend. "Hear what?"

Stacey looked back and forth between the twins. "About Jeremiah?"

"No, what?" Zeke said impatiently. He could tell Stacey was having fun drawing out the mystery.

"Well, last night he was sneaking around at the archaeology dig and he tripped over a rope in the dark. He broke his leg! One of the assistants at the dig drove him to the hospital. He was in the emergency room all night. I hear he's home now with a cast up to his knee."

"What was he doing at the dig in the middle of the night?" Jen asked.

Stacey shrugged. "I don't know. But I guess the two head archaeologists were pretty mad, especially since his mom is one of the protesters and the archaeologists are really fed up with them already. One of the archaeologists wanted to have Jeremiah arrested for snooping around."

Zeke looked at his sister. "If his last name was Smith, I'd really be wondering . . ."

". . . about the bad luck legend," Jen finished for him.

5

Whispered Secrets

After school, the twins headed directly for the barbecue at the dig site on their bikes.

"I wonder if the ghost will make another appearance today," Zeke said as he zoomed by Jen.

"Hey, wait up!" Jen shouted. They pedaled furiously down the rutted path that led into the woods, wound between trees, and finally exited at the dig site. They arrived at the dig in a record-breaking eighteen minutes, laughing and gasping for breath. They parked their bikes at the end of the path and headed around the dig to the camping area, where the college students were setting up a buffet.

On their way, Jen nudged Zeke. "Look, there's Mrs. Casely. What's she doing here again?"

Zeke stared at Mrs. Casely, who was strolling around the excavation area. Every once in a while, though, she took a quick look around before poking her cane into random mounds of dirt.

"Looks like she's searching for something," Zeke guessed. "I wonder if—" he began, when a sudden chant interrupted his thoughts.

"Go home! Leave our past alone! Go home!" the picketers shouted.

"They sure are getting louder," Jen commented, watching the picketers marching back and forth behind a yellow line of tape.

"And angrier, from the sounds of it," Zeke added thoughtfully. "I don't see Mrs. Blake, do you?"

Jen scanned the faces, then shook her head. "She must be home with poor Jeremiah."

"Poor Jeremiah?" Zeke repeated, lifting one dark eyebrow.

Jen grinned at her twin, her blue eyes sparkling with mischief. "I admit he wasn't poor Jeremiah when he was trying to run us off the road, but now I feel kind of sorry for him. Don't you?"

Zeke just rolled his eyes.

They started again in the direction of the barbecue preparations, but they were stopped by angry voices coming from the trailer. Jen put her finger to her lips and tiptoed closer. She'd recognized Professor Murphy's and Frank's voices. *What were they arguing about this time?* she wondered.

The dark green trailer rested off the ground on stacked concrete blocks. Three wooden steps at the back of the trailer led up to the door. The space under the trailer was used to store buckets and barrels and planks of wood that Jen guessed were used in the dig.

". . . at the press conference," Frank was saying.

Standing behind the trailer, with their ears practically glued to it to hear the conversation, Zeke felt very noticeable. "Come on." He pointed to a gap between the concrete blocks.

They quickly crawled through the opening and found themselves under the trailer. The grass was cool and cushiony. Most of the daylight was blocked out, but they could hear pretty well through the floor above them. They settled into kneeling positions.

". . . up to your old tricks," Frank was saying.

"It doesn't matter what you think," Professor Murphy answered. "I'll bet my career that you stole the knife! Now give it back."

Frank laughed. "You're crazy, you know that? No one even saw your precious knife. You wouldn't show it to anyone or even tell any of us what it was that you had found. You're just trying to pin something on me to get rid of me. Well, it won't work! Anyway, if the knife was so important, why did you lock it in this flimsy box for *safe*keeping?"

"What choice did I have?" the professor sputtered.

A moment later, the twins heard someone clomp over to the door. Heavy footsteps hurried down the stairs, leaving only one man still inside the trailer.

"Which one left?" Jen whispered.

"I couldn't see," Zeke replied.

Jen knew Zeke was thinking the same thing she was. They would have to wait to make sure it was safe to leave their hiding place. She didn't want to get caught and definitely didn't want Murphy to yell at her! She tried to find a more comfortable position in the soft grass under the trailer, but there was something digging into her right shin. Before Jen had a chance to fidget more, she was startled to hear someone going up the stairs and into the trailer.

She strained her ears to listen, but instead of loud, angry voices, now the two people were talking in hushed tones.

Zeke tilted his head to listen. He could hear a mosquito from twenty feet away. He was sure he heard a clinking sound.

Finally, a voice became clear and said, "That ghost stunt yesterday was great. I haven't been able to talk to you since then."

"It sure was. You did a great job."

"Me?" the other voice replied. "I wasn't the ghost. *You* were."

For a few minutes the voices became scrambled hisses. Zeke leaned over to tell Jen what he'd just heard, in case she hadn't caught it.

". . . getting suspicious!" one person said a little louder. "So be careful, whatever you do."

This was followed by the sounds of one person leaving the trailer. A few seconds later, the other person also left, and they heard a snap as the padlock on the door was fastened.

Jen waited as long as she could, then she peeked through the gap and scrambled out behind the trailer when she saw that the coast was clear. She couldn't stand another second of kneeling on that rock or stick under the trailer. She brushed the grass off her legs, realizing with dismay that she'd wiggled around under the trailer a bit too much, and now her knees were stained green.

"What's the matter with you?" Zeke asked, watching his sister rub her shin.

"I was kneeling on a rock or something," she said. "Did you hear anything else?"

"Just that someone is getting suspicious of them and they have to be careful."

"Did you recognize their voices?"

Zeke shook his head in frustration. "I couldn't even tell if they were male or female, though one of them must have been either Frank or Professor Murphy."

"And if one of them was supposed to dress up as the ghost, but neither of them did, that means there's a *third* person playing the ghost. But who?"

"Maybe the real ghost of the murderer?"

Jen shivered.

Suddenly Zeke realized that the worktables were unattended. He still wanted to look under the black plastic covering. "Now's our chance," he whispered, motioning toward the fourth table.

The twins casually walked over to the portable toilet near the canopied worktables. When they thought no one was looking, they scooted around to the back of the tables and crawled to the last one.

Very carefully, Zeke drew back the plastic. Empty eye sockets stared up at him!

6

A Ghostly Warning

Jen bit her lip to keep from crying out. Zeke stood frozen, staring back at the skull. When he'd thawed enough to move, he peeked under the plastic in another area. More bones. It didn't look like an entire skeleton, but there were at least five skulls and a number of other bones. Each one was neatly arranged and labeled.

"Where did they get these?" Jen hissed.

"They must have found them here. These must be the murdered settlers. The archaeologists probably keep the bones under cover to protect them and so the protesters won't be upset. Imagine what they'd do if they saw these skulls!"

"I thought skeletons were supposed to be white," Jen said, wrinkling her nose at the dirt-encrusted bones.

Zeke shook his head. "Not if they've been buried for over three hundred years."

Jen swallowed hard. "I've seen enough. Let's get out of here."

But Zeke wasn't ready. He tentatively poked a

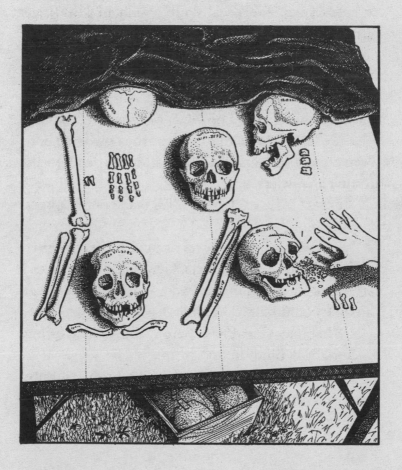

finger at the first skull. It rocked back and forth.

"Careful," Jen warned. "Why do you want to touch it anyway? That's totally gross."

Zeke ran his fingers over the cheekbone. "It's fascinating, though. When will I ever get another chance to examine a real skull?" Suddenly, his finger pushed through a thin section of the skull near the nose cavity, crumbling it to powder. He snatched his hand back.

"That guy didn't get enough calcium," Jen said, her voice trembling. "And now you've ruined the skull."

Zeke leaned forward to look at the powdered bone more closely. He scratched his nail over the forehead, leaving a powdery trail.

"It's fake!" he exclaimed. "It's made out of plaster or something!"

"And with all the plaster around for reconstructing bowls and other artifacts," Jen said, pointing to a large sack of the plaster powder stored at their feet, "anyone could have done it."

"What are you doing here?" snapped a furious voice right behind them.

They whirled around to face Professor Murphy. His lips were twisted into an angry line.

"We—" Zeke began. "I just wanted to see what was under here."

The professor snatched back the plastic and stared at the skull. "What have you done to it?" he demanded, keeping his voice low.

"I only touched it lightly and it fell apart. I think it must be a fake."

"Don't you dare say that! Get away from here right now!" the professor spat at them. A section of gray hair fell across his forehead. "You don't know what you're talking about! And if I ever see you two around this table again, I'll—" He took a menacing step toward them and they took off.

Jen's heart didn't stop pounding until they reached the barbecue area. "What is going on around here?" she exclaimed. "Bloody ghosts, missing murder weapons, crumbling skulls . . . sheesh! I haven't had this much fun since—"

"Oh no!" someone screeched right near them. This time it wasn't Lori. "The ghost is back!"

Sure enough, there it was, right where the ghostly apparition had appeared last time. The figure was wearing a hat, pants, and a bloody white shirt and held a long knife at the end of a menacingly upraised arm.

But something to its far right caught Jen's eye. When she turned to look, she stared in disbelief. There was a second ghost! Only this one looked like it was out for Halloween, wearing a white sheet with cutout eyeholes. It looked at the first ghost, did a double take, then fled back into the darkening forest. It all happened so quickly that Jen wondered if she had imagined it. Everyone else seemed to be focused on the bloody ghost.

"Staaaay awaaaaaaaay," the first ghost moaned. "Staaaaay awaaaaaay!"

"Creepy," Jen whispered.

The apparition slowly faded backward into the dark shadows of the trees. For a second, no one moved. Even the picketers were silent. Then, a moment after the ghost disappeared from sight, just like last time, Michael headed into the woods in pursuit.

"Come on," Jen urged. "We need to investigate, too."

The twins caught up to Michael just under the cool shadows of the trees. He was bent over and staring at the ground, apparently following a trail. He motioned for them to stay back. "I see a path going this way," he said over his shoulder.

Jen and Zeke followed a few feet behind him, noticing the overturned leaves on the forest floor and several broken twigs. After about twenty feet, Michael stopped, shooting fingers through his blond hair, making it even spikier than before. He looked around, obviously perplexed.

"This is exactly where the trail ended last time,

too," Michael began thoughtfully. "It's like the ghost ran right into this tree and vanished."

"But how could a ghost leave a trail?" Jen asked. "Don't they float *through* things?"

"Some spirits can disrupt earthly objects," Zeke said, "if the ghost is upset enough. I read that on a ghost, ghouls, and monsters Web site."

Jen and Zeke spread out, searching the ground for clues. Nothing.

"This dig is doomed," Michael said after a few more minutes of scouting. "Everyone is really upset about the two professors fighting all the time, and this ghost isn't helping to cheer anyone up." He gave up his search with a sigh and started back toward the camp site. "Coming?" he asked, motioning to the twins.

Jen reached out and held her brother back. "In a sec," she answered, ignoring Zeke's puzzled expression. As soon as Michael was out of sight, she pulled her brother in the direction of the second ghost, explaining what she had seen in that brief instant. "I don't think anyone else noticed," Jen finished. "Let's just look for any clues there."

They found an area of crushed underbrush and newly kicked-up soil. They followed the rough trail between trees until they lost track of it about fifty yards from where Jen had seen the second ghost appear.

Then, it was impossible to follow the trail any farther.

"I didn't see anything," Zeke said after they had retraced their steps and examined the entire path again. "But obviously, someone's been here."

"At first I thought I had imagined the second ghost, but it's too clear in my mind. Hey, look!" She ran over to a patch of prickly underbrush. Carefully, she pulled off a small square of white material they had both missed seeing.

Zeke looked at the cloth. The edges were frayed as though it had been torn by the underbrush from a larger piece. "Now all we have to do is find a ghost with a missing patch of skin and we'll have our culprit," he teased.

Jen shoved the bit of cloth into the back pocket of her jeans. "It's better than nothing."

"True," Zeke agreed. "But it still seems like we're getting nowhere on this case."

"We need more information if we're ever going to figure out what's going on—like what the bloody ghost is really up to, who dressed up in a sheet and pretended to be a ghost, and why Murphy won't tell Frank what he found if they're supposed to be working together."

"And don't forget about Jeremiah," Zeke added. "He must be involved in all this somehow, or why would he have tried so hard to keep us away from here?"

Jen nodded. "More clues," she said thoughtfully. "That's what we need." A second later she snapped her fingers.

Zeke's stomach dropped. Jen's snapping her fingers usually meant trouble.

"We have to look around in the trailer!"

"But it's locked," Zeke protested, reluctantly allowing Jen to lead him along in that direction.

Jen pulled a tiny screwdriver out of her pocket and held it up triumphantly. "Ta-daaa!"

"Where'd you get that?"

"Detective Wilson gave it to me from his new eyeglass kit when I said I thought it was cool." Jen grinned. "He already had one."

"I just hope you know what you're doing."

"Of course I do. No problem!"

"You got *half* of that right," Zeke muttered. "And it's not the *no* half."

7

Trapped!

As they left the edge of the forest, Jen and Zeke stayed hidden in the shadows and skirted the campsite. Preparations for the barbecue seemed to be stalled as everyone talked about the ghost.

From the shadows, Zeke noticed Lori scramble out of her tent and walk toward Michael.

Michael narrowed his eyes suspiciously at Lori. "Where were you? Hiding in your tent? I didn't hear you scream this time."

Lori glared at him. "Very funny."

"I'm quitting," one of the nearby workers said, looking around nervously as though the ghost might jump out at them. "This is too creepy with the ghost and the picketers shouting. I say we just leave this haunted place alone."

There were murmurs of agreement from several others.

Michael shook his head in disgust.

Zeke frowned. What the professors had most feared was about to happen. All the archaeology students would quit and the dig would be finished, just like the picketers wanted.

Jen and Zeke made their way toward the trailer. The protesters began to chant again.

"Look, Mrs. Blake must not be taking care of Jeremiah after all," Jen commented, nodding toward Jeremiah's mother.

Zeke walked over to her and got her attention. "Sorry to hear about Jeremiah's broken leg. I hope he's okay."

"He'll be fine as soon as these meddlers leave!" Mrs. Blake snapped angrily. "We'll all be. Go home! Leave our past alone!" she shouted toward the group of students at the barbecue.

Zeke winced as the loud voice pierced his eardrums. Just as he was about to turn away, he noticed that one of Mrs. Blake's fingers was bleeding. He pointed it out to her. "I think I have a bandage in my backpack," he offered.

Mrs. Blake just stuck her wounded finger in her

mouth. "I'm fine," she said curtly.

Shrugging, Zeke mumbled good-bye and the twins hurried back toward the trailer, nearly crashing into Frank.

Frank steadied Jen and smiled at her. "Watch where you're going or you could get a black eye."

Jen blushed. "Sorry. I hope I didn't step on your foot or anything," she said, looking at Frank's new work boots.

He lifted his foot, showing off the clean orange of the leather. "New boots with steel toes. Can't feel a thing. Now keep your eyes open." With that last bit of advice, he strode off toward the long tent that covered the worktables.

At last, the twins reached the back of the trailer and crept up the three steps to the door. Jen took a deep breath and studied the rusty chain and the newer-looking padlock that kept the trailer safe from thieves. Well, not all thieves, she reasoned, since someone had gotten in and stolen the knife from Professor Murphy's hiding spot.

She gripped the padlock in her left hand and prepared to pick the lock with her right. But the lock swung open. She stared at it.

"It wasn't secured," Zeke said. "I wonder who left

it open? I'm sure I heard it being locked before."

Jen quickly slid the chain free and unlatched the door. They darted into the semi-dark trailer. The blinds had been drawn, and the sun was low in the sky.

After a moment, their eyes adjusted to the dimness. They split up, and Jen searched one end of the trailer, while Zeke searched the other.

Zeke flipped through three file cabinets stuffed with folders. Nothing jumped out at him as suspicious or important. He peeked behind the cabinets for anything that might be hidden there, but it was too dark back there to see clearly.

"Zeke!" Jen exclaimed, trying to keep her voice down. "Look at this!"

Zeke scrambled over to his sister. In the dim light he looked at a small metal lockbox that was shoved off to the side of the desk. A stack of papers partially hid it from view.

"See? The lock is busted," Jen said, pointing. "Think this is where Professor Murphy hid the knife?"

Zeke reached out a hand. "Maybe. Is there anything in there?" He carefully lifted the top of the box. The hinges squeaked. The box wasn't empty. He stared into it. "I didn't hear the professors talk about this. Someone must have just put it in here."

They stared at a knife tucked into the box. Even in the limited light, Jen could tell the sharp blade was covered with sticky red liquid, just like blood. "This can't be the one that Professor Murphy found. It looks too new."

Zeke nodded in agreement. "It's definitely a fake and the blood looks like barbecue sauce. What's written on that piece of paper?"

Jen peered closer at the note that was taped to the inside of the lid. *"Leave now, or else!"* she read out loud. "Someone definitely wants everyone out of here."

"So the real knife was stolen, and someone put this new, bloody knife in its place, obviously as a scare tactic."

"I'll bet no one's found it yet," Jen said, "or we would have heard about it. We're the first ones to see it. Should we tell someone?"

"And admit we were in the trailer?" Zeke said. "Not a good idea. We have to leave and let someone else find the knife."

Jen thought about it for a moment. "You're right. Just close the box like it was before. We'll sneak out and wait until someone comes in here and finds it. I bet it'll cause a lot of trouble. Maybe we'll be able to tell who hid it here by seeing which person acts the least surprised."

Zeke lowered the lid of the box, wincing when it squeaked. From outside the trailer door came a familiar sound of something clinking together. Before either one of them could wonder what it was, the door to the trailer slammed shut.

Stunned, the twins listened as someone rammed the lock into place. They were trapped!

8

The Bloody Knife

Jen's heart pounded in her chest like a jackhammer. She stumbled to the door and tried to open it. The door rattled, but wouldn't open. "We're locked in!" she whispered. "How are we going to get out of here?"

Zeke held up his hand. "Don't worry, we'll find a way out."

"Someone knows we're in here," Jen went on. "We could be in big trouble for trespassing."

"At least we don't have to worry about the police. I don't think the person who locked us in will want the police involved if they had anything to do with stealing the knife and putting this fake in its place. Whoever it is will definitely think of another way to get rid of us."

"Oh, great," Jen replied. "Let's call for help out the windows."

"No way. Then everyone will know we were sneaking around. And we can't let anyone know we're trying to figure out this mystery." Zeke closed his eyes, thinking hard. "We have to escape without anyone seeing us. When we were under the trailer, I noticed a little door above us," he said slowly. "It could be an escape hatch, like a fire exit." He got down on his hands and knees. "Help me look for it. It's our only hope of getting out of here . . ."

. . . *alive*, Jen finished silently for him, gulping back a moan. She dropped to her knees and ran her fingers across the gritty floor.

"I think I found it," Zeke said.

Jen hurried over to him, feeling the outline of the trapdoor. "Here's the handle," she said, lifting a small metal ring and tugging.

"Pull harder," Zeke ordered.

Jen squatted and got a better grip on the ring. She yanked as hard as she could. With a creak of protest, the door loosened and flew open. Jen fell backward.

"Great! You did it," Zeke exclaimed. "Now let's get out of here."

The opening was small, and Jen didn't know how an adult would ever be able to slip through it. But she could get out and that's all she cared about at that moment.

The ground was only three feet away. She squirmed through the opening to the grass below and crawled off to the side so her brother could escape, too.

Zeke dropped his backpack to the ground. Then he grabbed the trapdoor as he slithered through, meaning to close it after him. But something jammed the door and it wouldn't shut all the way.

"Hurry up," Jen hissed, anxious to get away from there.

"Just a sec," Zeke hissed back. He ran his fingers around the frame of the door. A scrap of something

must have been on the floor when Jen opened the trapdoor and it had gotten caught in the hinge. He pulled it loose and gave the torn piece of paper a quick glance, but it was too dark to read what was written on it. He shoved the scrap into his pocket, then lowered the door over his head.

"Let's get out of here," Jen said.

Zeke nodded, moving after her. "Ow, I just hit that rock you were kneeling on before," he said, trying to rub his knee with one hand and feel around in the soft grass with the other.

Jen checked to make sure the coast was clear and was about to scramble out from under the trailer, when Zeke gasped.

She turned. "What is it?"

Slowly he held up a dirty object. "This is what you were kneeling on before," Zeke said. "It's the missing knife!"

"Are you sure?"

Zeke nodded. "It looks like it was just dug out of the ground. Whoever stole it from the professor hid it under the trailer. They probably dropped it through the trapdoor."

"That means they'll come looking for it later," Jen said with a shiver. "What should we do with it?"

"We have to return it to Professor Murphy."

"And admit we were snooping around? He's already mad at us for looking at the bones."

Zeke removed his clean sweatshirt from his backpack, wrapped it around the knife, then carefully put the bundle in his backpack. "Let's just take it and worry about what to do with it later, after we do some more investigating."

Jen bit her lip, not sure this was the best idea. Whoever stole it would be looking for it. And if he or she found out they had it . . . She refused to think about that. They scrambled out from under the trailer, walking away from it as quickly as they could. They didn't want anyone to notice them anywhere near it.

Jen peered around. Michael and Lori were talking to several of the archaeology students, and Frank was lingering nearby. Professor Murphy was nowhere to be seen.

"Let's go talk to Michael and Lori," Zeke suggested. The delicious smells of barbecued chicken started to drift their way.

The junior archaeologists were talking about which historic site they'd most like to dig up.

"How about Atlantis?" Lori said dreamily.

Michael snorted. "You and everyone else."

"Why do you have to be like that?" Lori huffed.

Michael threw up his hands. "Like what?"

"So negative. Just wait, I'll be a famous archaeol-ogist someday!" With that, she flounced away.

Michael grinned ruefully. "I'm always saying the wrong thing," he said to the twins. "But I don't know why she's so touchy—" A shout of fright interrupted him.

Michael whirled around. "The ghost again?" he exclaimed. But there was no ghost to be seen.

Lori came running from the direction of the trailer. "It's in there!" she screamed, her voice high in terror.

Jen and Zeke glanced knowingly at each other.

Michael grabbed Lori by the shoulders as she raced by. "What? Is the ghost in there?"

Lori shook her head frantically. "No, the bloody knife is!"

At that moment Frank rushed over to them. "What's wrong?"

Lori shivered. "There's a bl-bloody knife in the trailer," she stammered. "Oh, it was awful."

Professor Murphy joined the group. "Now what is it?"

But everyone was already heading toward the trailer. "What is it?" he kept demanding.

Jen and Zeke stood outside the trailer with the others while Frank and Professor Murphy charged up the rickety stairs and disappeared inside. A moment later they came out. Professor Murphy was carrying the box with the knife in it.

"You did this!" he yelled at Frank. "You stole the real knife and put this fake in my lockbox."

"I certainly did not," Frank shouted back. "You're the one more likely to do something like that," he said, his voice full of scorn. "Or maybe it was the protesters. They'd love to scare us all away."

Professor Murphy showed the waiting group the bloody knife. "Who did this?" he demanded.

No one answered. Michael stepped forward for a closer look. "This is just a knife anyone could buy at a department store," he said. Then he leaned forward and sniffed. "Smells like barbecue sauce," he added.

Zeke nudged Jen in the side.

Michael turned to Lori. "Are you sure this isn't one of your tricks?"

"No way!" she exclaimed. "It scared the wits out of me. Why would I do something like that?"

Michael shrugged, but he kept staring at Lori as some of her friends took her toward the campfire area to calm her down. The two professors went back inside the trailer, still arguing, though it was impossible to hear their exact words.

Jen turned to Michael. "Who has a key to the

trailer and might have planted that?" she asked.

Michael gave a short laugh and pulled out a ring with tons of keys on it. He jingled it. "It's a joke. *Everyone* has a key to the trailer. Anyone could have planted that knife in there. Someone probably thought it would be a good joke since Professor Murphy's knife got stolen."

"Doesn't seem that funny to me," Zeke said.

Michael grinned. "Archaeologist humor. Sometimes we put fake bones in each other's sleeping bags."

"Ugh," Jen said. "That doesn't sound funny at all."

"I'd better go see how the professors are doing," Michael said, heading into the trailer. "See you later."

"He didn't seem too surprised about the knife," Jen commented as soon as he was out of earshot.

Zeke agreed. "But why would he do it?"

Jen couldn't come up with an answer, so she finally said, "Maybe we'll think better after we eat. The food sure smells great."

Zeke readily agreed. They headed for the barbecue and loaded their plates with coleslaw, three-potato salad, chips, and chicken that was crisp on the outside and moist and juicy on the inside. The food was so delicious it was hard to think about anything else until it was time to go home.

There was still a faint blush of light in the sky as the twins rode home. When they reached the B&B, Jen and Zeke parked their bikes and hurried around the back of the building to the kitchen door. They were passing under a giant maple tree, when something fell on Jen's head.

"Hey, there's my Snurf ball!" she exclaimed, chasing after the foam sphere and picking it up. "Where'd it come from? I've been looking all over for it."

Slinky, the twins' cat, meowed from up above in one of the tree branches.

Zeke laughed. "That sly cat had it hidden in the tree."

Jen looked up. "Sheesh, I searched all over the ground and in the bushes, but I never thought to look up," she admitted. She waved the ball at her cat. "Thanks, Slinky."

When the twins entered the kitchen, Aunt Bee was having dinner with Detective Wilson.

"Stacey phoned a little while ago, Jen," Aunt Bee called after Jen as the twins headed out of the kitchen to wash up.

The twins went to their rooms to change out of their dirty clothes. Zeke put the backpack, with the knife still inside, in a corner of his closet. Then he dropped his dirty shorts and T-shirt into the hamper. Glancing around to make sure everything was neat, he left his room and met Jen in the museum on the first floor of the lighthouse tower. He took one look at his sister's face and knew something was wrong.

"I just called Stacey. She wanted to talk about the next soccer game. But then she mentioned that Jeremiah's little sister fell off the monkey bars at the playground. She broke her arm!"

Zeke frowned. "First Jeremiah's accident, then his sister's. That's a lot of bad luck for one family. It sounds an awful lot like the bad luck curse. I have a feeling that if we don't hurry up and figure out what is going on at the dig site, there will be a lot more accidents," Zeke said somberly. "And they might not end with just broken bones."

9

The Scandal

The next day was Saturday. Jen and Zeke headed to the dig early in the morning. They were still not sure who should get the knife, so they left it home. As soon as they pedaled into the clearing, they could tell something was seriously wrong. Jen noticed that the colored ropes that marked off areas of the dig site had all been messed up, and the neat piles of dirt had been scattered. Large gouges of earth had been removed from other areas, as though someone had been frantically looking for something.

Even the tables with the artifacts looked vandalized. The objects weren't lined up in straight rows anymore, but were scattered at random and some had fallen to the ground below. Zeke noticed the bone table was still covered with the black plastic, though.

"I'll bet someone was looking for the knife," Jen said.

The twins hurried over to Michael and Lori, who were surrounded by a group of upset college students. "It was probably some townspeople just trying to ruin the dig," Michael was saying. "After all, the knife we found last night was obviously a fake, and the blood on it was just barbecue sauce. They want to scare us away from here."

"But now it'll take us all day to reorganize everything before we can start more excavations," Lori wailed.

"Okay, everyone back to work," Frank said, striding up to the group. Jen noticed his new shoes were already grass stained across the tops. It seemed like everything got dirty at a dig. "No time to waste," Frank went on. "The press conference is tomorrow, and we have a lot of work to do to straighten this place up and give a good impression, especially with Murphy's reputation." The students scattered, heading in different directions. Michael went with them, giving instructions along the way. Only Lori and Frank were left.

Frank turned to the twins. "I have to ask you two to leave. After what happened last night, we can't allow any outsiders in the area."

"What about the picketers?" Zeke asked.

Frank looked at the crowd of protesters. "They have to stay behind that yellow line. There's nothing we can do about them." He walked off without looking back.

Lori frowned after him. "He's not usually so cranky," she said to them. "But you'd better get going. If Professor Murphy sees you, he'll be really upset. He's *always* in a bad mood."

"Why does Frank keep mentioning Professor Murphy's reputation?" Zeke asked.

Lori opened her mouth to answer when someone snapped, "What are these kids doing here?" They all turned to see Professor Murphy charging toward them. "Get out of here!"

Jen and Zeke took off before the professor reached them. "Do you think he was the one who locked us in the trailer?" Jen asked as they ran toward their bikes. "He sure doesn't seem to like us. Maybe he hoped to lock us up and keep us out of the way."

"Maybe," Zeke agreed. "I think if we find out what scandal he was involved in, it will help us figure out what happened to the missing artifacts."

They reached the edge of the clearing where they had parked their bikes. Jen was already on hers when Zeke said, "I just want to check one more thing." Without giving Jen a chance to argue, he started off toward the long tables. He needed one quick peek at those old bones. He had a suspicion about something, but needed a closer look.

As he walked toward the covered table, Zeke kept a watchful eye out for Professor Murphy. The minute he reached the covered table, he dropped to all fours. When he reached the bones, he rose up on his knees, lifted the black plastic, and stared right into the eyes of a skull. The cheekbones were there—nothing had crumbled to dust. Nervous but determined, Zeke reached out with a sharp stick and scratched the skull along the forehead. The dirt scraped away, leaving a bright white, chalky line. Another plaster skull! It wasn't the same one that he'd already ruined. Someone had replaced that one with *another* fake.

Zeke inched down the table, testing each skull and bone. Two more pieces revealed plaster under the dirt. He didn't have time to test them all, but he guessed that at least half the bones were fakes.

He hurried back to Jen, who was chewing on her lower lip. She only did this when she was worried.

"I thought you were going to get caught!" she exclaimed. "Let's get out of here!"

"What are you two doing?" a familiar voice demanded.

Jen bit back a cry of surprise. "Jeremiah!" she

exclaimed. "Where did you come from?"

"I'm here with my mom, protesting."

"On crutches?" asked Jen.

"Yeah, so what." Jeremiah sulked.

"Did you and the other protesters mess up the dig site?" Zeke asked him.

"No way," Jeremiah said.

"Well, everyone thinks the protesters are to blame," Zeke warned him. "If Frank or Professor Murphy catch you here again, you'll be in big trouble."

"It's a free country," Jeremiah said stubbornly. "I have a right to be here. It's these stupid archaeologists who should go home."

"Why do you even care?" Jen asked.

Suddenly Jeremiah whirled around on his crutches and headed in the direction of the protesters. Soon he was lost from sight.

"What spooked him?" Zeke wondered.

Jen tugged on his arm and pointed. Professor Murphy was heading toward them, a dark glare in his eyes. "Let's get out of here!"

As fast as they could, they jumped on their bikes and pedaled away from the dig. When they knew they were safe, Zeke told Jen what he'd discovered under the plastic.

"Why would someone try to pass off fake bones as

real ones? They're bound to be discovered as soon as someone starts to examine them more closely."

Zeke lifted one shoulder. "Good question. I have a feeling it's all part of the mystery and the old curse."

~⁀~

After lunch, the twins had a few hours free before they had to clean the guest rooms.

"Be back by three," Aunt Bee called after them as they escaped out the door.

"Okay," Jen called back. They hadn't found anything about Professor Murphy's scandal on the Internet, so they were headed for the town library to search for information.

They hopped on their bikes and coasted down the long driveway to the winding road that led into town. They took the old logging road to town instead of riding around Dead Man's Curve—a sharp curve on Coast Road, where the cliff suddenly dropped off to the rocks and ocean below—which was totally scary.

At last they reached the outskirts of Old Mystic Village, the older part of town. They rode down Main Street, heading for the library. Suddenly Zeke jammed on his brakes. Jen nearly ran into the back of him.

"What are you doing?" she demanded, righting her bike.

"Did you see him?" Zeke asked, ignoring his sister's anger.

"Who?"

"Michael." Zeke got off his bike and leaned it against the brick wall. He peeked into the Mystic Café window. Jen followed.

"Who's he talking to?" she whispered, hoping Michael wouldn't look up and see them spying on him. They watched as the assistant archaeologist signed a paper and then shook hands with the stranger. They both stood up and Michael looked around uneasily.

Jen and Zeke scooted out of sight. They waited a second, then peered in the window again. Michael and the other man stood up, laughing about something, and they headed separately for the exit.

The twins jumped on their bikes and rode on.

"What do you think that was about?" Jen wondered as they parked their bikes at the rack in front of the library. From there, they watched as Michael headed uptown toward the road to the dig, while the stranger drove out of town. "He looked really guilty."

"Lori said he was up to something," Zeke added.

They entered the library and asked the research librarian for assistance. Aunt Bee had been the head librarian for years and years, so Mrs. Shaker asked about her as she led them to a file of microfiche.

"Here we have old issues of *Archaeologist Digest* on film. Insert it in that machine over there, and you can look at the contents and see what issue and page you are interested in looking up. Good luck."

Jen sighed. Research was not her favorite thing to do, especially on such a beautiful day.

Zeke inserted a film and scanned through it. He pointed to a heading that read, "Scandal at the Mississippi." The subheading read, "Murphy fakes artifacts."

10

Another Suspect

Quickly, Zeke twirled the dials to find the article. The twins read silently.

Jen, a faster reader, sat back on her chair, waiting for Zeke to finish. When he did, he turned to his sister. "Wow," he said.

"No wonder he has such a bad reputation," Jen said. "He faked all those artifacts at that dig along the Mississippi and got caught."

Zeke nodded. "The article said he did it for more fame and because they weren't finding anything very important. If they didn't hurry up and find something really great, the dig was going to be closed down."

"Maybe he's trying it again at this dig," Jen suggested.

"I'll bet he faked that skull," Zeke said quickly. "Remember how mad he got when he caught us and

I told him the skull was a fake?"

"But why would he fake artifacts at another dig? It will completely ruin his career."

"That's probably why Frank is so upset with Professor Murphy. He's worried that if the professor fakes something, no one will believe either of them again."

"Unless Frank can prove that he had nothing to do with the fake artifacts," Jen countered. "And then with Professor Murphy out of the way, Frank would be in charge of everything."

"Or maybe one of the protesters knows about the professor's past and is trying to ruin the dig by planting fake artifacts. Tomorrow is the press conference," Zeke said thoughtfully. "It will be the perfect time to reveal a scandal."

"Could Michael and the stranger have anything to do with the fake artifacts?" Jen wondered out loud. "Maybe Michael was signing something to prove the professor is guilty of faking things again. With Murphy out of the way, Michael might get his job and Lori would take Michael's place. Everyone would get bumped up."

Zeke tapped his finger on the table. "It seems like everyone has a motive for getting Professor Murphy out of there."

"But knowing that doesn't help us solve the mystery," Jen said with a sigh as they returned the film to the file drawer. "It does mean we probably shouldn't return the knife to Professor Murphy, though. Maybe the knife is a fake, too."

Zeke agreed. "So there are two possibilities. One is that Professor Murphy is faking the skulls himself and doesn't want to get caught. The other is that someone else is faking the artifacts and wants to blame it on Professor Murphy."

"We just have to figure out which one is right and who is to blame," Jen said. She made a face. "No problem!"

Outside, she took a deep breath of the cool Maine breeze, enjoying the warmth of the sun on her face. They rode along slowly, each one pondering all the clues.

When they passed the public Laundromat, they saw a familiar brown ponytail inside. Jen called out to Lori and the twins waved at her when she turned around.

"Laundry day," Lori said, smiling. "It feels good to wash all the dirt out of my clothes. It's even in my sheets. Ugh! I can't stand a dirty pillowcase."

"Don't you have an extra set of sheets?" Zeke asked, thinking about how Aunt Bee kept four sets of sheets for every bed in the B&B. That way there were always clean sheets available, even if the wash didn't get done on time.

"Actually, I did have an extra set," Lori admitted, "but one sheet was stolen."

Jen and Zeke exchanged a look. *Stolen? By the person who wore it to look like a Halloween ghost?*

"So what are you two up to?" Lori asked.

"Just riding around," Zeke answered. No need to let on that they knew about Professor Murphy's scandal. After all, Lori worked for him and might not appreciate their investigating him.

"We have to go," Jen said, staring across the street.

Zeke looked to see what had captured his sister's interest. *Smith Sisters Salon*, read the peach-and-blue sign over the door.

"Bye, Lori," Jen said as she pedaled away.

Zeke waved at Lori and rode up next to his sister. "This isn't the way home," he said.

"I know, I just have to check something out." In front of the salon, Jen jumped off her bike and leaned it against the wall. "Back in a sec," she said as she disappeared through the front door.

A few minutes later, she reappeared, a worried look on her face.

"What's wrong?" Zeke asked.

Jen shook her head and didn't answer until they were well away from the salon. Finally, she said, "Guess who the Smith sisters are."

Zeke shrugged.

"Betty Zane is one of the sisters, and Jeremiah's mom is the other. Smith was their maiden name. They could both be direct descendants of Obadiah Smith!"

Zeke gasped. "Of course! I knew the last name Smith rang a bell. No wonder Mrs. Blake is so upset about the dig, especially now that Jeremiah and his sister have both had accidents."

"The legend really could be coming true," Jen agreed. "And if the legend is real, maybe the ghost is, too."

"If we don't get to the bottom of this, the accidents are going to keep happening."

They rode the rest of the way home in silence. At last they fought their way up the long, steep driveway to the B&B. When they got inside they found that Aunt Bee had all the cleaning supplies out and ready for them to start cleaning the rooms.

"This will give us a chance to take a peek into Mrs. Casely's room," Zeke said as they started the cleaning. "There must be a reason why she's at the dig all the time. I don't think it's just for rest and relaxation."

When they got to the Rose Room where Mrs.

Casely was staying, they took extra care to keep their eyes out for anything suspicious. While dusting, Zeke even checked behind the pink-and-yellow-rose-printed curtains, and under the chair that was striped in similar colors.

Jen picked up the small rose-patterned waste basket. But when she dumped the contents into the plastic trash bag they carried from room to room, a few slips of paper fell to the floor. As Jen picked them up, she noticed that one paper was small—a business card.

She looked it over, then handed it to her brother, who stared at it in amazement.

Julianna Casely

Ambrosia Antiques

New York, NY

Specializing in Early American Artifacts

Zeke flipped the card over. Written in red pen were the words *Avon University*.

"Isn't that the university sponsoring the dig?" Zeke asked after he showed it to Jen.

"I think so."

"Could she be trying to steal the knife for her antiques store?"

At that moment Zeke heard someone heading for the room—someone who walked with a steel-tipped cane!

11

At Midnight

The door swung open and Mrs. Casely stared at them, her pointy nose looking even more pinched than usual.

"Just finishing up in here," Jen said with a wide smile. Tying a knot in the garbage bag, she quickly followed Zeke out of the room. She could feel Mrs. Casely's eyes burning holes in her back, and she didn't take a breath until they were around the corner.

Jen flopped against the wall. "That was close!"

"What was close?" Aunt Bee said, marching past with an armful of laundry.

"Uh, I almost knocked into Mrs. Casely with the broom," Zeke said quickly.

Aunt Bee eyed them. Zeke was grateful that, even though she might sometimes be suspicious of what they were up to, she didn't question them. "I'm doing laundry now. Please get yours and bring it down," Aunt Bee requested as she started back down the hall.

Jen groaned. Now she'd have to hunt all over her room for dirty socks and T-shirts. Zeke left Jen in her messy room on the second floor of the lighthouse tower and kept climbing the stairs to his room on the third floor. It would only take him a few minutes to collect his dirty clothes from the hamper and bring them down to Aunt Bee. Then he'd have to wait another hour for Jen—unless he helped her, as usual.

Zeke sorted through his clothes, making sure all the pockets were empty and the socks right side out. He found two quarters, a piece of gum, and a scrap of paper in the shorts he'd worn yesterday. Shoving the gum in his mouth, he inspected the paper, suddenly remembering it had been wedged in the trapdoor of the trailer. Finding the knife right after getting out of the trailer had completely put this note out of his head.

Avon U dept. of forensic
anthropology lab
203-555-7865

Zeke frowned. Avon University again—the school sponsoring the dig. But what was forensic anthropology? He grabbed his dictionary off the bookshelf and read that forensic anthropology had to do with identifying skeletal or biological remains. He snapped the dictionary shut and hurried down to Jen's room.

As expected, she was still pulling dirty socks out from under her bed. She was sprawled on the floor with only her legs sticking out. He tapped her on the back to get her attention. Surprised, she jerked her head up and howled with pain. Then she scrambled free of the bed, rubbing her head. "I wish you wouldn't sneak up on me like that. All I can think about is that awful ghost."

Zeke tried to cover a laugh. "Sorry, but this is important. Look." He showed her the scrap of paper.

"Let's call," she said right away. "Maybe it has something to do with the fake bones."

They hurried down to the front desk and placed the call there. When they finally got through, a lab technician asked for the code or file name.

"Uh," Zeke said, looking at Jen, who had her ear next to the receiver, too.

Jen shrugged and mouthed, "Mystic murders?"

"Mystic murders," Zeke said, keeping his voice low so he'd sound older.

"Oh, right, here it is. All the tests were done. Let's see, no marks on the bones, but the bowls—hey, who is this? This file is marked confidential. Are you—?"

Zeke hung up the phone.

"Why'd you hang up so fast?" Jen cried. "The guy was about to say someone's name. The name of the thief, I'll bet!"

Zeke realized his mistake and frowned. "If I call back he'll just get more suspicious. I can't believe I did that. I panicked."

Jen grinned. "You? Mr. Calm, Cool, and Collected?" She laughed and leaned out of the way when he threw a playful punch at her. Then she turned serious. "What did he mean by no marks on the bones?"

Zeke sat back on the couch and stared up at the ceiling. "No marks on the bones," he repeated. "But something about the bowls."

"So whoever took the bones and replaced them with fakes must have also stolen bowls."

"And maybe the same person also stole the knife and hid it under the trailer!"

"We have to go to the dig and do some more sleuthing," Zeke said. "Tonight. It'll be perfect because there's not supposed to be a moon."

"Can't we go in the daylight?" Jen asked, already knowing the answer. Not that she minded the dark. But with the ghosts and skulls, the dig wasn't her first choice for a dark, moonless night.

Zeke firmly shook his head. "No way. Someone might see us. I'll come to your room to get you at midnight."

~⌣~

Jen tried to keep her eyes open, but when Zeke knocked on her door, she'd fallen fast asleep and Zeke had to wake her. She stumbled into the stairwell, wearing blue jeans and a black hooded sweatshirt, and carrying a flashlight.

"Wait till you hear what I found out on the Internet," Zeke said, sounding excited.

"What?"

"Shhh," Zeke warned. "I'll tell you when we get there."

They tiptoed downstairs and out the kitchen door. Jen had her house key in her pocket. Silently, they wheeled their bikes along the path into the fields before turning on their bike headlights and climbing on. Zeke rode in the lead, shining his flashlight far down the path so they wouldn't somersault over any rocks or fallen logs.

Jen shivered, telling herself it was because of the cold air, not fear. Animals scampered through the underbrush as they rode along, startling the twins every ten feet or so. It seemed to take forever to reach the final bend in the path. They jumped off their bikes at the dig site and lay them down, ready for a quick getaway, if necessary. Then, holding their flashlights low to the ground, they crept toward the canopy tent where the bones were stored.

Zeke kept his eyes on the light bobbing in front of him so he wouldn't trip and make a sudden noise. If someone caught them tonight, they would be in huge trouble.

At last they reached the table of bones. Zeke lifted the plastic and shined his light across the skulls. Some of them still showed faint scratches from his earlier tests. He chose several bones that were real, not molded plaster, and examined them carefully under the light.

"Do you see anything?" he whispered to Jen.

Jen held her flashlight close to the bones and peered at them. "Nope, they just look like dirty things to me."

"How about here?" Zeke asked, showing her a few more bones.

"No. What am I looking for?"

"Any weird scratches or notches?"

Jen looked more closely. "Nope."

Zeke smiled. "Exactly. There are no signs of violence. Remember the guy at the lab said there were no marks on the bones?" he whispered.

Jen nodded.

"I couldn't figure out what that meant, but I knew it had to be important. So I checked it out on the Web. There are always cuts or gouges on the bones of people who have been stabbed. Even after all these years, there would be some sign on these bones if the people had been murdered by a maniac with a knife."

"Wow. Then how did they die?" Jen snapped her fingers softly. "The bowls!"

Zeke nodded. "Food."

"Poison!"

A twig snapping to their left seemed to crack like a gunshot.

Jen and Zeke flicked off their lights. The twins crouched, ready to flee. Another footfall came closer.

Jen grabbed Zeke's hand and pulled him farther back into the shadows. In the inky darkness, they saw a hooded figure slowly creeping toward the bone table. It was too dark to see who it was.

The person lifted the black plastic, took several skulls and bones, and dropped them into a bag. Then the person replaced the items with new ones and crept away.

Jen's heart was pounding about a million beats per second, but she had to know what the shadowy figure had just done.

Without a word, she crept toward the skeleton table, pulling Zeke along with her. When they reached it, Zeke lifted the black plastic. Jen flicked on her flashlight, right into the empty eye sockets of a skull. The light wobbled in her hand, but she bit back her cry of alarm. After all, it's not like she didn't know what she'd be seeing.

Zeke poked at the first skull. Then he scraped his nail along the ridge of the eyebrow. Nothing flaked off. The plaster skull had been replaced with a real one!

12

The Chase

Quickly, Zeke checked the other skulls and bones. All the fakes were gone!

"Let's get out of here," Jen whispered. A shiver of unease trickled up her back. Something didn't feel right.

As soon as they had moved away from the tables, Jen saw what it was. A figure with a flashlight was coming right toward them.

The twins scuttled away in the direction of their bikes. The flashlight darted after them. The figure started to run.

Jen jumped on her bike and pedaled down the dark path. As soon as she rounded the first bend, she flicked on her flashlight so she wouldn't run into anything.

"That was close," she said.

No one answered.

A jolt of fear electrified her. She jerked around, swinging her flashlight frantically. Zeke wasn't behind her. He was nowhere in sight. For a split second she debated what to do. Go home and get help and maybe get grounded forever? Or go back and rescue Zeke alone?

It wasn't much of a choice. She decided to try to find Zeke on her own first. If he'd been caught, or if he was hurt, she'd have to get Aunt Bee.

Trying to steady her breathing, she turned her bike around and slowly, carefully rode back to the campsite. As she got closer, she turned off her flashlight and hopped off her bike and pushed it, trying not to disturb the underbrush.

"Psst!"

Jen froze.

"Jen, over here!"

"Zeke?"

Zeke crawled out from under a bush. "I wanted to see who was chasing us, so I hid."

"Who was it? Did you see?"

"It was Michael!"

"What was he doing?" Jen asked, keeping her voice softer than a whisper.

"I'm not sure. He went over to the tables and flashed his light on everything, then he went back to his tent."

Jen felt a smile tug at her lips. "I thought maybe the ghost had gotten you."

Zeke shuddered. "Don't even say that! Now come on, we'd better get home."

The farther they got away from the dig site, the more Jen's tense shoulders eased. But she didn't feel completely relaxed until they were safely in her room.

"So," Zeke said, flopping onto Jen's inflatable chair. "We know Michael was the second person, but who was the first one, the one wearing a hood?"

"I thought you had it all figured out," Jen responded.

"Suspect sheets," they both said together. Jen grabbed a pen and several sheets of paper. Half an hour later, she read aloud what they had come up with.

Mystic Lighthouse

Suspect Sheet

Name: Lori Taylor

Motive: With Professor Murphy gone, she might move up to a more important position.

Clues: She's the only one with a cot and regular sheets and the sheet could have been the second ghost. Was one extra sheet really stolen?

MICHAEL SAID SHE WASN'T SO INNOCENT. WHAT DID HE MEAN?

COULD SHE HAVE BEEN THE ONE TALKING TO ONE OF THE PROFESSORS IN THE TRAILER ABOUT BEING A GHOST?

Mystic Lighthouse

Suspect Sheet

Name: Michael Durnes

Motive: Wants Professor Murphy's job?

Clues: WHY DOES HE KEEP INVESTIGATING THE WOODS AFTER THE GHOST DISAPPEARS? IS HE TRYING TO COVER UP EVIDENCE?

Who was he talking to in town? What was he signing? It looked suspicious.

WHAT WAS HE LOOKING FOR ON THE BONES TABLE WITH A FLASHLIGHT TONIGHT?

Doesn't get along with Lori.

Doesn't seem to get along with his boss, Prof. Murphy. Could he be trying to ruin the dig to get back at him?

COULD HE HAVE BEEN THE ONE TALKING TO ONE OF THE PROFESSORS IN THE TRAILER ABOUT BEING A GHOST?

Mystic Lighthouse

Suspect Sheet

Name: Professor Murphy

Motive: Wants fame?

Clues: IS HE FAKING ARTIFACTS AGAIN AND TRYING TO SCARE EVERYONE AWAY FROM THE DIG SO THEY DON'T FIND OUT?

WHO STOLE THE KNIFE HE FOUND? OR DID HE PLANT IT UNDER THE TRAILER HIMSELF?

Was he the one left in the trailer? If so, who was he whispering with about being a ghost?

DID HE SEND THE BONES AND ARTIFACTS TO THE AVON U. LAB? WHY?

Mystic Lighthouse

Suspect Sheet

Name: Frank Pruitt

Motive: Seems to dislike Professor Murphy and doesn't want him around. If he gets rid of Murphy, he'll get all the glory.

Clues: Fighting with Prof. Murphy in public.

Did he steal the knife? If so, why?

Was he the one left in the trailer? If so, who was he whispering with about being a ghost?

After the ghost sighting, he was coming from the trailer. Did he plant the bloody knife?

Mystic Lighthouse

Suspect Sheet

Name: Mrs. Casely

Motive: Trying to get artifacts to sell in her store?

Clues: She owns an antiques store. Why didn't she tell us the truth about who she is?

Why is she around the dig so much?

Did she somehow steal the knife and hide it and hope to get it later?

Why does her business card say Avon University on the back?

Mystic Lighthouse

Suspect Sheet

Name: Jeremiah Blake and his mother

Motive: His mom's last name is SMITH! So they are cursed, according to the legend. Want to ruin the dig.

Clues: Jeremiah threatened Zeke. He almost ran us over.

DID HIS MOTHER STEAL THE KNIFE?

Did she leave the bloody one to scare everyone away from the dig?

WAS HER FINGER REALLY BLEEDING, OR WAS IT SAUCE FROM PLANTING THE FAKE KNIFE?

Jeremiah was around the dig after it was vandalized. Did he do it?

Zeke shook his head. "No one seems completely guilty. What are we missing?"

Jen frowned, trying not to yawn. "I don't know, but whatever it is, it'll have to wait till morning. I can't think anymore."

Note to Reader

Have you figured out who is causing all the problems at the dig? Jen and Zeke have made pretty good notes on the suspects, but they did miss a few very important clues. Without those clues, it's almost impossible to figure out who is trying to ruin the dig.

Have you come to a conclusion? Take your time. Carefully review the suspect sheets. Fill in any details Jen and Zeke missed. When you think you have a solution, read the last chapter to find out if Jen and Zeke can put all the pieces together to solve *The Mystery of the Bad Luck Curse*.

Good luck!

Solution

Another Mystery Solved!

Jen could barely crawl out of bed the next morning. Twice while preparing the breakfast buffet, Aunt Bee had to remind her not to pour the milk into the OJ pitcher.

"You've got dark circles under your eyes and you look very pale," Aunt Bee finally said. She felt Jen's forehead. "Are you sick?"

"No, I'm fine," Jen said. "I didn't sleep well last night, that's all."

As soon as the meal was over and the twins had cleaned up the kitchen, they took off for the dig. They didn't want to miss the press conference. They knew that everything would probably reveal itself today.

"Did you bring the knife?" Jen asked as they ran out the door.

Zeke nodded. "It's right here, in my backpack. I have a feeling we'll need it."

Jen shivered. "It sounds deadly when you say it like that."

When they reached the site, they hurried to the platform that the newscasters had set up for the press conference. The archaeologists stood chatting in groups. Jen could feel the tension in the air.

As the time neared one o'clock, people began to settle into chairs that had been set up in front of the platform. Jen nudged her brother. They both watched as Jeremiah Blake hobbled to a chair and sat down. He didn't look at the twins. Frank and Professor Murphy stood behind the cluster of microphones on the platform.

"They sure didn't dress up for this," Zeke said.

Jen nodded, noting the dirty shoes and dirt-stained pants. "I guess they want to look like real archaeologists."

A woman tapped her watch as the signal, and cameras started whirring. Frank cleared his throat. "Welcome to Mystic, Maine. We are trying to unearth the mystery of what happened to the early settlers in this area. In 1698, twenty-three settlers were viciously killed here, and—"

Professor Murphy leaned toward the mike and interrupted Frank. "Actually, what you just said is not completely true."

Frank stared at Professor Murphy. Then, with an icy edge to his voice he said, "Would you like to explain yourself? Or maybe this is one of the forgeries you're so well known for?"

Before Professor Murphy could respond, an eerie wail came from the far side of the camp. Without even glancing in that direction, Jen and Zeke knew what they'd see. Sure enough, there was the bloody ghost, waving a knife at them. "Go awaaaaay! Goooo awaaaaaay!" it moaned.

"Come on," Zeke said, suddenly realizing there was something very wrong with this supposed ghost. He shot out of his chair, not looking to see if Jen had followed.

He ran around the dig site, careful not to mess up any of the piles of dirt or the colored ropes that had been neatly rearranged after yesterday's vandalism. At the edge of the woods, he hesitated only a second. The ghost had disappeared the instant Zeke had started to run.

Jen was panting when she caught up with him. "What are you doing? Are you nuts?"

"It was talking," Zeke panted out. "The ghost in the legend isn't supposed to talk. Remember? We read that on the Internet."

"You're right," Jen said slowly. "So it can't be the real ghost—not that I ever thought it was real," she added quickly.

"Right," Zeke said thoughtfully. "But that doesn't explain how the ghost disappears into thin air."

By this time, not only had Michael caught up to them, but the two professors, Lori, and a number of reporters holding mikes and cameras had also followed them between the trees. Jeremiah hobbled after them, too.

With Jen and Zeke in the lead, they traced the ghost's path to where it dead-ended. They searched the ground.

Suddenly Jen stopped. "Remember my Snurf ball?" she asked Zeke. Everyone stopped to look at the twins.

Jen looked up into the tree that stretched toward the sky above her. She pointed. Everyone gawked as they looked up into the branches of the tree. The bloody ghost was crouched on one of the limbs.

"Mrs. Blake!" Zeke exclaimed. "You're the ghost?"

Mrs. Blake sighed and nimbly climbed down the tree. She moved next to Jeremiah and put a hand on his shoulder. "I was just trying to scare everyone away. There have already been two accidents in my family, and my sister cut her hand with the hair clippers yesterday. The curse is coming true!"

"And I was trying to scare you two off," Jeremiah admitted, his eyes downcast. "I've heard you're good at figuring out mysteries, and I knew that if you kept at it, you'd find out we are part of the cursed Smith family. Then you might realize it was my mom pretending to be the ghost and you'd ruin everything before we scared the archaeologists away."

Mrs. Blake looked down at her bloody costume. "This is just ketchup," she admitted. She glanced at Zeke. "I had some on my finger and you thought I was bleeding. Thanks for offering the bandage anyway. And I'm really sorry about all the commotion I caused. I was just so worried about my family, especially when the accidents started. I thought for sure the bad luck curse was coming true."

Zeke quickly explained to everyone that Jeremiah's mom used to be Miss Smith, the many times great-granddaughter of Obadiah Smith, the only survivor of the legendary murdered Mystic settlers.

"Were all the protesters descended from Obadiah?" Jen asked.

Mrs. Blake shook her head. "Oh no. They were just concerned citizens who felt that someone's final resting place shouldn't be disturbed, especially since they were all murdered."

"That is not entirely true," Professor Murphy interjected. "There was no murder."

A flurry of whispers circulated.

"What are you talking about?" Frank bellowed. "We have the scattered bones to prove it. If this had been a regular settlement, the bodies would have been buried in an orderly fashion."

Zeke raised his hand to interrupt. When everyone looked at him, he took a big breath. "Actually, Professor Murphy is right. The bones show no evidence of the legendary murder."

Everyone stared at him in shocked silence. Finally, one of the reporters asked, "How do you know?"

"I checked the Internet to find out what to look for," Zeke explained. "Then I examined a lot of the bones from this dig and found no nicks or marks on them that would show that any of the people had been shot or stabbed. They died from something else."

"Exactly!" Professor Murphy crowed. "They died of food poisoning."

"What?" Frank sputtered. "You're crazy. You're just up to your old tricks again."

Professor Murphy narrowed his eyes. "You know very well that I didn't fake those artifacts all those years ago. You were my assistant on that dig!"

"You can't prove anything."

Professor Murphy waved the issue aside. "That was all so long ago. All I want to prove now is how these poor settlers died and show there never was a vengeful ghost or a bad luck curse of any kind. I had the bones examined at the forensic anthropology lab at Avon University. As the boy said, there are no signs of violence on the bones. I also took some of the cooking artifacts—"

"So you *were* stealing!" Frank interrupted. "I bet you stole your own knife from the trailer and tried to blame me!"

Jen nudged her brother. Maybe this would be a good time to reveal the knife. But he shook his head.

She shifted uncomfortably and looked down at everyone's feet. People fighting always made her uncomfortable. And it was clear one of the professors still had something to hide, but which one?

"I did not steal my own knife," Professor Murphy shot back. "You did. I just can't prove it."

Jen remembered kneeling on the knife under the trailer a few days earlier. "Hey," she suddenly said before she even realized she was going to speak. "I know who stole the knife, and I *can* prove it."

Zeke looked at her, puzzled. This was news to him.

"Zeke and I were, uh, scouting around, and we found the missing knife under the trailer. Someone must have dropped it through the trapdoor in the floor to pick up later. We took the knife, thinking we should return it to Professor Murphy, but we never found the right time to do it." She decided it was better not to admit that they didn't trust him.

"But the next day," she continued, "someone had vandalized the dig. We think it was to look for the missing knife." Jen slowly eyed the crowd. Her gaze finally rested on Frank. "You did it. You were the one to steal the knife from Professor Murphy."

"That's crazy," Frank sputtered. "Why would you think that?" Jen pointed to his boots. He laughed. "My feet? What do they have to do with anything?"

"Those are brand-new boots," Jen explained to everyone. "I remember they were perfectly clean the day before the vandalism because I bumped into you and you told me they were new boots with steel toes."

Frank scowled. "So?"

"Look at them now," Jen instructed.

Frank laughed shortly. "They're dirty. What a surprise. We are on an archaeological dig, you know. Things usually do get dirty."

"But not grass-stained on the *tops*," Jen pointed out, "unless you were on your knees in the grass under the trailer, looking for the missing knife."

Everyone stared at Frank's boots.

"Good going, sis!" Zeke cheered. "I never would have figured that out."

Jen smiled at him. "That's okay. You figured out the mystery of the bones." She turned back to Frank. "So, I'm right, aren't I? And you vandalized the site looking for the knife, too, right?"

Frank scowled at her. "I deserved to find that knife," he blurted out. "I wanted to unveil the murder weapon at this press conference. But when it disappeared from under the trailer where I hid it, I went crazy. I looked everywhere, but I couldn't find it."

"Excuse me," Professor Murphy interrupted, looking at the twins. "Does this mean that you two have the knife?"

Zeke nodded and carefully pulled his rolled-up sweatshirt out of his backpack. He unrolled it to reveal the knife. "Here you go."

The professor examined it closely for a second, then smiled. He held up the old knife and spoke to the crowd. "I believe this is the knife that cut the spoiled food. The lab found traces of deadly bacteria on the bowls and several spoons. I found this knife near the cooking area. If it is the one that came in contact with the bacteria over and over again, it should have high traces of it on the blade. This will confirm my hypothesis."

"You mean that wasn't the murder weapon?" Frank said dully.

"You said it was," Lori accused him. Everyone turned to look at her. "You said we'd look like heroes when we revealed the murder weapon at the press conference and Professor Murphy would look bad, and I'd get a higher position and . . ." Her voice trailed off as she realized she'd said way too much.

"So you were the Halloween ghost in a sheet," Zeke said, nodding thoughtfully. "You were working with Frank, probably trying to create a diversion so Frank could plant the bloody knife in the trailer. But you weren't counting on Mrs. Blake to make her ghostly appearance at the same time. Jen saw you run away, but you left a patch of your sheet behind, which is why you only have one complete set of bedsheets."

Jen nodded in agreement.

"And now I remember the clink of your bracelets when you were whispering with Frank in the trailer."

Lori scowled at them. "I knew you two were nosing around too much."

"You locked us in the trailer!" Jen exclaimed. "We

heard the jingle of your bracelets then, too."

Lori looked confused. "Wait, what are you talking about?"

Jen paused. "You mean you didn't lock us in? It was right before the barbecue."

Michael stepped forward, looking thoughtful. "Actually, that must have been me. I had no idea you were in there, though. I saw the trailer unlocked so I locked it up for safekeeping." He pulled the large set of keys out of his pocket. "You must have heard these."

"Are you working with Frank and Lori, too?" Zeke asked.

Michael's eyes widened. "No way!"

"Then who was that man you were talking to at the Mystic Café?"

Michael took a step back and ran a nervous hand through his hair. "Oh, you saw me?"

The twins nodded.

"To tell you the truth, that was the man who hired me for my new job. I've been trying to get another job, as Lori knew. I thought all her hints about it would get me fired before I found a new position. I knew there was weird stuff going on at this dig, and I didn't want my career ruined in case Professor Murphy was, uh, faking artifacts again. And since I'm his head assistant, it wouldn't make me look too good."

"But I never faked *any* artifacts," Professor Murphy repeated. "As I said, Frank was my assistant long ago, and I'm sure he was the one faking the artifacts to make me look bad. He wanted to get me fired and take all the glory for himself. Unfortunately, it worked. But I could never prove it."

Michael shrugged. "I didn't know that then. I believe you now, though." He looked at Frank. "Now that I know all the facts."

"What were you doing snooping around last night?" Zeke asked.

Michael looked surprised. "How did you know about that?"

Zeke looked sheepish. "Uh, we were kind of scouting around then, too."

Michael laughed. "I thought I heard a noise, but when I didn't see anyone, I figured it was just a raccoon or something. I checked the tables with the artifacts just to be sure, but everything seemed to be in order."

"So you weren't the one who put all the real skulls and bones back under the tarp?" Jen asked.

Michael raised his eyebrow. "What are you talking about?"

Professor Murphy cleared his throat. "I'm afraid

you saw me. I knew you kids were aware of the fake skulls because I caught you looking at them. I tried to scare you off from snooping any more, but obviously that didn't work." A small smirk turned up his lips. "I made plaster castings of some of the skulls and bones so I could send the real ones to the university lab for testing without anyone missing them. I didn't need to do that with the pottery shards I took, though, because they hadn't been cataloged yet, and I knew no one could completely prove they were missing. Last night I replaced all the plaster castings of the skulls and bones with the real items."

"I knew some of the pottery shards were gone," Lori said. "I couldn't figure out why anyone would want them, though."

Jen turned to her. "So you were in on this whole scheme with Frank. But what did the bloody knife have to do with anything?"

"That was Frank's idea," Lori said, giving Frank a dirty look. "He said the bloody knife would make it look like the protesters had stolen the real knife and replaced it with the fake one. He bought a really cheap knife and used barbecue sauce for the blood because he thought that's what a protester would do. He said if we used a good fake, Professor Murphy would know that one of the picketers couldn't have done it."

"Be quiet," Frank muttered darkly. "You've said enough already."

Lori glared at him. "If I hadn't listened to you in the first place, I never would have been caught up in this mess." She turned back to the reporters. "He told me how much he hated Professor Murphy because Murphy had all the luck in finding artifacts. Frank was so jealous, he decided to ruin Professor Murphy's reputation years ago. The bad publicity worked for a while, but when he got paired up with Professor Murphy on this dig, he got really upset. Frank said he'd ruin Professor Murphy's career once and for all."

Zeke shook his head. He heard the regret in Lori's voice, but he didn't think that would help her when she tried to get another archaeology job. And Frank's career was definitely ruined.

"What did Mrs. Casely have to do with all of this?" Jen wondered out loud, trying to get everything straight in her mind.

"Me?"

Surprised, Jen realized that Mrs. Casely must have joined the group without her noticing.

"I am a specialist in Early American artifacts. Avon University hired me to keep an eye on this dig.

They were concerned, especially when they heard things had started to disappear."

The twins nodded. It all made sense now.

One of the reporters shook her head. "This is the most fascinating press conference I've ever been to!"

"But what about the curse?" Mrs. Blake asked. "No one got murdered, so you mean there isn't one?"

"I'm glad to say there is no curse," Professor Murphy said. "Your ancestor survived because he didn't eat any of the poisoned food."

"Which, if you think about it," Zeke pointed out with a grin, "is actually *good* luck!"

About the Author

Laura E. Williams has written more than twenty-five books for children, her most recent being the books in the Mystic Lighthouse Mysteries series, *ABC Kids*, and *The Executioner's Daughter*. In her spare time she works on the rubber art stamp company that she started in her garage.

Ms. Williams loves lighthouses. Someday she hopes to visit a lighthouse bed-and-breakfast just like the one in Mystic, Maine.

Mystic Lighthouse

Suspect Sheet

Name:

Motive:

Clues: